Zero into Plus

A Philosophical Drama in Three Acts

Rajeshwar Prasad

TSL Drama

First published in Great Britain in 2025
By TSL Publications, Rickmansworth

Copyright © 2025 Rajeshwar Prasad

ISBN: 978-1-917426-38-1

Cover courtesy of :
https://pixabay.com/illustrations/barrier-tape-city-evening-curfew-5821997/

Zero into Plus

(A philosophical drama in three acts)

Yearly religious celebrations are held in Alietland. Free food and lodging facilities are provided by Aliet Charitable Trust. JAY and RAY are sitting in the office of the Trust. They discuss the importance of charitable works in the life of man, God, life, people, and the world.

Characters

JAY	75 years old, director of 'Aliet Charitable Trust' in Alietland
RAY	65 years old, the honour of several companies
DON	40 years old, is a notorious criminal who robs and kills during the religious celebrations
NEWSREADER	[On the television screen.]

Running Time

68 minutes

Setting

The office of 'Aliet Charitable Trust' in Alietland.
Bills and vouchers, tables and chairs, etc.

Act 1

Lights up.

Director JAY is sitting in his office. RAY joins him. They are talking about charity and its importance in life and religion.

An announcement is heard. 'Pilgrims, attention, please! There is free food and lodging available from Aliet Charitable Trust. All are requested to avail themselves of the vegetarian food and lodging facilities'.

JAY: [*Sees* RAY.] Most welcome in this office of charity!

RAY: Thanks a lot!

JAY: Please take a seat.

RAY: Thanks again.

       [*Sits.*]

JAY: Please tell me if there are any problems.

RAY: No. Everything is fine.

JAY: Really?

RAY: Yes. Quite fine!

JAY: Very good! The man of values and virtues!

RAY: I have come to discuss the rest of the expenses for these celebrations, and have **already donated one million dollars.**

JAY: Fine. The details of expenses are on the table to discuss for further preparation.

       [*Shows some documents.*]

RAY: Nice. Let us discuss it. Don't show it.

JAY: But first, I want to show you the bills and vouchers of previous expenses against your donations to the trust.

RAY: Don't worry. This is not an issue. I will see it later.

JAY: But I want to show all this to you as I did in the past.

RAY: Let it go. I will look at it in the future.

JAY: Okay. But everything should be transparent.

RAY: I know and understand.

JAY: It is my duty to maintain transparency.

RAY: Let it go. Think about the future. I am quite able to face any expenses for yearly religious celebrations.

JAY: I know.

RAY: I will continue to do so lifelong.

JAY: I know and understand it but it is better to give the bills and vouchers for previous expenses. You must credit the second instalment after it.

RAY: Really, this is not an important matter for me, but it is to provide more funds for the charitable works in this city of God.

JAY: The previous night the accountant had calculated and said that a heavy fund of one million is balanced in our account which is sufficient for six hours.

RAY: It means you need a sufficient amount for the next eighteen hours.

JAY: Yes! Absolutely!

RAY: How much amount do you need?

JAY: It needs proper calculation which is now not possible because the accountant is busy with the management of charitable works.

RAY: No matter.

JAY: I will submit the bills and vouchers for all the expenses and the final account of all this.

RAY: Okay...okay.

JAY: Now you can credit whatever you like but I suggest you deposit at least one million dollars.

RAY: Okay.

JAY: Please submit the cheque.

RAY: Give me an accurate amount.

JAY: Donate one million dollars.

RAY: Verify once again.

JAY: [*Verifies. Files in hands.*] Okay. It is right. It is sufficient. If I lack, I will ask you for more donations.

RAY: It is right?

JAY: Absolutely. Take it.

[*Signs and gives the cheque.*]

RAY: I feel pleasure doing so.

JAY: I know and understand. We all appreciate your gentle-mindedness.

RAY: God has blessed me for it.

JAY: Only because of some great men has the world survived.

RAY: I don't feel that I am a great man – I feel that this is my duty towards the country and its people.

JAY: People have not lost faith in life only because of some great men and their grand works.

RAY: Absolutely.

JAY: If not, it would not be an easy task to manage any works of charity in the country. You are a great man. I honour your greatness.

RAY: [*Silent.*]

JAY: Greatness must be honoured.

RAY: This is our sacrament, so I follow like all others.

JAY: Humanity is hidden in it.

RAY: The charitable works of man help him to wash away sins.

JAY: All say. It is an eternal mystery.

RAY: Whatsoever but a man always tries to discover the ways to God.

JAY: All say and try.

RAY: I ever remain ready for such charitable works only for these reasons.

JAY: The whole city praises you for such works.

RAY: I will continue my work here as usual. Now I wish for a successful ending.

JAY: If a great man like you is dedicated to the works of charity, no problem will occur. Everything will happen well. Half of the programme has been finished and with your donation, the rest will also be finished successfully.

RAY: I feel my responsibility and duty.

JAY: This is your greatness.

RAY: Not my greatness, but my duty.

JAY: This shows your super greatness that you feel this is a duty.

RAY: Whatsoever.

JAY: I am right.

RAY: I donate millions of dollars each year on such occasions only because of your encouragement.

JAY: All know your contribution to the celebration.

RAY: I don't mind all this.

JAY: Your contribution is seen in every part of the city and seen even in the dust of the streets. All know it.

RAY: But possible only because of God.

JAY: Millions of people eat each year during the celebrations in the free camp arranged by you.

RAY: I am quite helpless. All this is possible only because of God's mercy.

JAY: It credits your virtues. It shows your super greatness.

RAY: This is the way to win the blessings of God.

JAY: The entire country knows your works of charity.

RAY: But all by God's blessings. Not only in this city but rather in every fair, for familiar religious celebrations and in the centres of people gathering I do such work and I spend millions of dollars each year. It is by and of God's award.

JAY: All praise your works everywhere.

RAY: Even a leaf can't move without His will.

JAY: Every man defines it differently.

RAY: But the truth is always out of question.

JAY: Yes. You are right. But the truth is always ignored. This is also another fact.

RAY: This is fact but it does not mean that one can devalue truth and God, Who is the only truth.

JAY: All say that there is God – they believe God. Some say that he is connected to Him and he declares himself as a godman. I have listened to all this.

RAY: All this is an absolute truth.

JAY: But none witnesses Him and dies waiting for Him.

RAY: There is no question whether there is God or not. God is everywhere. This is not a matter for question.

JAY: But I have firm faith that there is no God in this universe.

RAY: How do you say all this?

JAY: As I feel.

RAY: You should consider what you are saying.

JAY: Natural things are naturally expressed. None can control this passion.

RAY: Is this a natural idea that you condemn the existence of God?

JAY: I don't condemn God or His existence, but the makeup and consequent events of the world condemn God and His existence automatically.

RAY: You are a responsible person, so you should not talk in such a manner.

JAY: I feel all this.

RAY: Really, you are a well-known person in the city and you have arranged charitable works for the visitors and devotees on such occasions for the last twenty years.

So, you have enough knowledge and experience of religion and its values in the life of man and the world. You also know the way of man to God.

JAY: Really, you are a man who has done so many charitable works. So, you must know all this.

RAY: Undoubtedly.

JAY: You have much experience and knowledge regarding such matters.

RAY: Okay.

JAY: But you have seen the depth of what happens to a man who does such works?

[*Shows a two-minute video of gods and goddesses on his mobile phone.*]

RAY: [*Silent.*]

JAY: Can you?

RAY: I have thought very deeply about all this. I know all this.

JAY: What?

RAY: God is without a doubt. We all are at His mercy here and there. He is our supreme commander.

JAY: How?

RAY: See and feel God and His effect on this world and people.

JAY: Have you ever considered that people themselves accept the existence of God and condemn too?

RAY: I have considered it deeply. None condemns. All accept His existence. None says that there is no existence of God.

JAY: All condemn.

RAY: None.

JAY: All...all. Think deeply.

RAY: No...no.

JAY: You are living in a state of illusion – a hundred per cent confusion.

RAY: How?

JAY: All know it. All ignore it.

RAY: What?

JAY: There are different faiths, sects, and cults. Do you?

RAY: Yes.

JAY: All this is the challenge against the existence of God.

RAY: No.

JAY: Yes, I am quite right.

RAY: How?

JAY: Each religion gives freedom to everyone to live and practice his faith in his own way.

RAY: That is a fact.

JAY: Thus, all these challenge the existence of God – the existence of other faiths.

RAY: How?

JAY: This is an important matter which you must consider.

RAY: What is the matter?

JAY: The real matter is that different faiths, cults, and sects are burns and wounds on the existence of God.

RAY: How?

JAY: They challenge the existence of God.

RAY: Tell me. How?

JAY: [*Long pause.*] How many eyes are there to man?

RAY: Two.

JAY: If I say three – if one says four – if another says five – if the other says six. Is all this right or wrong?

RAY: All this is wrong.

JAY: But different faiths, cults, and sects are considered true and right by a particular group of people, and for others that is wrong. If I may? How can you justify that all are right? For one which is wrong and for another the same is right. How?

RAY: Man used to follow all this from generation to generation – from age to age. So, we all believe in God. We all do the same which was done by our forefathers.

JAY: Either we believe God or not – it is a different matter. The main matter is that we believe Him without any proof and because this is a matter of belief – this is a matter of faith.

RAY: Faith is the sea of life.

JAY: But life is absurd – faith is absurd.

RAY: Is faith absurd?

JAY: Yes. Absolutely?

RAY: You are quite wrong.

JAY: I am absolutely right.

RAY: How?

JAY: Because faith is the ferment or setting of the cosmos and we are living here in its net.

RAY: No. We can easily see and feel the existence of God in the world.

JAY: That is a dream or illusion.

RAY: How?

JAY: God is the name of hope – of that hope which is never fulfilled.

RAY: [*Silent.*]

JAY: God is the name of absurdity. Man lives in expectations – another after one – one after one – but it is never fulfilled.

RAY: Expectations and their fulfilment are also God's will.

JAY: No...no!

RAY: You must believe it! Everything is commanded by God.

JAY: Know and believe. There is no God. God is not a truth but an illusion. God is an expectation.

RAY: God awards joys and sorrows.

JAY: God has nothing to do with joys or sorrows – God has nothing to do with life and death.

RAY: You denounce God.

JAY: No.

RAY: Really, you disregard Him.

JAY: I don't disregard anyone.

RAY: Then why do you say all this?

JAY: I say what is absolutely right.

RAY: You are not right.

JAY: You must believe it! I am right.

RAY: Know! Even a leaf can't move without God's mercy. God is supreme. God is our commander. He is supreme.

JAY: All this is your illusion. There is no God.

RAY: God is the only truth in this cosmos and except all this all are false. All are shadows on which all mankind moves and lives and finally departs from here for the House of God.

JAY: [*Laughs.*] Ha...ha.

RAY: Why do you laugh?

JAY: [*Laughs loudly.*] Ha...ha...ha.

RAY: I think you are disregarding me.

JAY: No...no.

RAY: I feel.

JAY: I really respect you.

RAY: It seems now.

JAY: Believe me. I am a man who never disregards anyone. But the setting of the world disregards all.

RAY: How?

JAY: Every success of a man is awarded by death. Death is the eternal award for all.

RAY: This is not a matter.

JAY: What do you feel?

RAY: You are a well-known person to me and I have warm regards for you.

JAY: I know.

RAY: I am now surprised.

JAY: Why?

RAY: You have been in my circle for the last twenty years and you have been performing charitable works in the city. So, your opinion should be mature.

JAY: My opinion is quite mature. I say only that I know and understand.

RAY: No. Think properly.

JAY: Believe, a millionaire man! The pride of the country!

RAY: How can I believe your meaningless ideas?

JAY: Know. My ideas are fully matured. I am saying what is true, though none accepts and waits for God. But He never comes and the man dies leaving everything usually.

RAY: If you are not ready to accept the truth, I can say nothing.

JAY: Please believe...believe. I am quite right.

RAY: No. You should learn to respect others' ideas too.

JAY: I am sorry. My motive is not to hurt you but to disclose what is in my heart and mind.

RAY: [Silent.]

JAY: I am always fair and practical. I don't believe in God, rather I follow what all others do – whether God exists or not.

RAY: What?

JAY: I do which I see, not because I believe. All are the same and do the same.

RAY: [*Surprisingly.*] Really, I am surprised at your attitude now.

JAY: Which attitude?

RAY: I have never seen this type of attitude in you in the last twenty years.

JAY: No.

RAY: Really?

JAY: What do you think about me?

RAY: Today what has happened to you?

JAY: Nothing.

RAY: Really, now you are in a new mood and temperament?

JAY: Nothing new has happened to me or my mind and heart. Everything is old and told. Everything is known and done. But despite all this, man always moves in the state of darkness and none can go leave this state. It is an eternal state. This is the puzzle of the world.

RAY: Is this a puzzle?

JAY: Yes. This puzzle is eternal.

RAY: But you never told me any of this in the past. I donate millions of dollars to your charitable trust, each year.

JAY: [*Long pause.*] Everything is under the control of time. None is out of the way. All situations pass on this track and everyone has to follow whatever is to happen.

RAY: But I believe that there is certainly God and without Him, there is nothing in this universe.

JAY: All believe without any doubt, thinking that God will give them something which is expected. But in fact, there is no God.

RAY: If there is no God, why do you work for pilgrims for the last twenty years?

JAY: Not only for twenty years, but I have passed my whole life in different ways in such works thinking that I will once see God – I will once meet God.

RAY: Have you?

JAY: Never.

RAY: See. Feel. God is everywhere.

JAY: I never see or feel God and I remain in the same condition as I was in the past.

RAY: Do you go to the holy place for prayer?

JAY: Yes. I go there each year for the Lord's blessings but I never witness Him and now I expect that I will never see Him. I have grown old in such manners.

RAY: But I see and feel God daily – I witness everywhere. Whatever I think, God awards me.

JAY: Nothing is awarded by Him. He is nothing. He is only an expectation.

RAY: But if there is no God, why do you do charitable works for the pilgrims each year and for this, you work night and day?

JAY: Like others – more or less.

RAY: You sacrifice your peace and rest for charitable works.

JAY: Everyone does as per his knowledge and capacity. This is a tendency. This is natural.

RAY: But you do all this very eagerly.

JAY: All do, seeing others according to one's knowledge and capacity. So, I also do this.

RAY: It means to say that you do not believe in God.

JAY: There is no God, so I don't believe in Him.

RAY: It means that your work of charity is only to pass time or life – only to continue the system.

JAY: Yes...yes.

RAY: But I believe God. I salute God, Who has given me everything – Who has given me a sound body and good health – who has given me all the things available in the world.

JAY: [*Silent.*]

RAY: I thank God, Who has given me enough property and that I am the richest man in the country.

JAY: That is nothing. That is zero.

RAY: Do you not know me?

JAY: What?

RAY: I sleep on the money. Gold and diamond coat every item of my house. I eat off a gold-made dish. My bed is made of gold and diamond. My buttons are made of diamond. See it now.

JAY: [*Laughs.*] Ha...ha.

RAY: [*Looks at him.*] Why?

JAY: Heh...made of earth.

RAY: Do you not recognize gold and diamond? It is possible only because of God's blessings.

JAY: I know all – I recognize well.

RAY: Then why do you laugh?

JAY: You are a minor boy.

RAY: Please don't insult me.

JAY: Please don't take it otherwise.

RAY: You must know it.

JAY: I know.

RAY: What do you know?

JAY: All is meaningless.

RAY: You must learn to respect life and wealth.

    [*Long Pause.*]

JAY: Firstly come to the dining table and eat the holy food made for the pilgrims and devotees.

RAY: Thanks.

    They leave.

    Lights down.

Act 2

Lights up.

JAY *and* RAY *once again come and sit.*

An announcement is heard. 'Pilgrims, attention, please! There is free food and lodging available from Aliet Charitable Trust. All are requested to avail themselves of the vegetarian food and lodging facilities'.

JAY: Really, you have a definite mindset like all others. So, you don't like to accept the bitter facts of life and the world.

RAY: I know well. I am not an illiterate man.

JAY: You miss knowing the real meaning of life.

RAY: I know it well. I know the importance of property in life.

JAY: You must believe. You don't know.

RAY: I know it well. My property increases daily. There is always plus never a minus. I only follow plus and plus. My whole family enjoys heavenly pleasure.

JAY: Man moves around plus but it automatically continues to change into zero.

RAY: I have added every item to my life. I enjoy every pleasure in my life. I have turned my life heavenly. It is possible by money and all this is only because of God's blessings.

JAY: [*Laughs.*] Ha...ha.

RAY: Why?

JAY: Ha...ha.

        [*Continues.*]

RAY: Why do you laugh?

JAY: How the entire world is in the darkness of ignorance!

RAY: How?

JAY: Man doesn't know even a minor thing.

RAY: What do you want to say?

JAY: I want to say that whatever you gain is totally meaningless. That is zero. You only see, but when the time comes all this will go in vain – all this will be turned into zero.

[*Shows a two-minute video of a massive causality in a temple who went to worship.*]

RAY: No.

JAY: You will continue to see everything, one by one, will disappear before your eyes. God will not come to save you – your property will not save you. All is in vain – they are only to see, not to use at the proper time.

RAY: You are wrong.

JAY: How?

RAY: I use and enjoy all that which I have made. I use all that and pass my life in pleasure, not in poverty like others. I am the richest man in my country and I feel proud of saying this.

JAY: You don't enjoy, rather you lose all this minute by minute. You are nearing death. You are nearing that grave that is long-awaited by four elements – earth, water, air, and fire.

RAY: Know! I make nine into nine and my property increases on this geometrical formula.

JAY: [*Laughs.*] Ha...ha

RAY: [*Silent.*]

JAY: [*Continues to laugh.*] Ha...ha...ha.

RAY: Tell me, what do you want to say?

JAY: You will not understand my ideas.

RAY: Why?

JAY: You are surrounded by all false things of the world and all this will not let you go out of the state of meaninglessness.

RAY: Am I surrounded by false things?

JAY: Yes.

RAY: Yes?

JAY: Yes...yes.

RAY: How?

JAY: All things in this world are mortal – all are false. Only one thing is true.

RAY: What?

JAY: Death.

RAY: Death?

JAY: Yes.

RAY: And life?

JAY: False.

RAY: Other things?

JAY: All are false.

RAY: In which world do you live?

JAY: In the same world.

RAY: In which all others live?

JAY: Yes.

RAY: No.

JAY: Yes...yes.

RAY: How?

JAY: Whatever you possess is of zero value. Items are absurd. They need not be possessed by us. They are like a mirage that disappears over course of time.

RAY: I always try to plus one more thing daily as all do it to the best of their knowledge and capacity.

JAY: Whatever you earn or make is totally meaningless. The

meaning of everything is 'zero into plus'. Your work of 'plus' is also under this universal formula. You cannot leave this order of the cosmos. The world runs on this formula. None can ignore this fact.

[*Shows a 2-minute video of the death of several rich people due to the Covid-19 virus.*]

RAY: I don't understand your ideas.

JAY: None understands all this.

RAY: What?

JAY: None understands this. So, you will also not understand.

RAY: None?

JAY: Really...none.

RAY: This is not a matter. I am a doctorate in Mathematics and Business. I have enough knowledge of all this. I can understand it easily and this is not my problem.

JAY: What do you want to know?

RAY: Make it clear.

JAY: What?

RAY: What do you mean to say by 'zero into plus' which is absolutely meaningless? I know its value in mathematics. Its value is zero.

JAY: You know its mathematical value and I know.

RAY: Right.

JAY: But you don't know its practical value in life which is your failure.

RAY: What do you want to say now?

JAY: I want to say that whatever you have made or earned, all that is zero. Life is zero. God is zero.

RAY: Life is not zero or absurd but full of pleasure. Man has come here by God's will. God has sent us here.

JAY: [*Laughs.*] Ha...ha.

RAY: Do you?

JAY: God has not sent us here. There is no God.

RAY: Then how have we come here?

JAY: Here we are in an irremediable exile. We don't know our home – we don't know our past, present, or future. We are aliens here. This is not our home – our home is unknown.

RAY: This is our home.

JAY: This is not our home. Our home is quite unknown.

RAY: This is our home and we are the most perfect beings who have come here at God's mercy.

JAY: This is the home for all beings except man.

RAY: Are we homeless?

JAY: Absolutely.

RAY: No.

JAY: You are living in an illusion. You don't understand its reality.

RAY: I do understand. I know and perform accordingly.

JAY: You don't know.

RAY: I know.

JAY: Believe. You don't know.

RAY: Do you like to blur the facts?

JAY: No.

RAY: But I feel.

JAY: You are living in an illusion like all others.

RAY: How?

JAY: You say that you plus something daily – but that is really nothing. That is zero. You should know the mathematical formula of life. The world runs on 'zero into plus' and all men have to follow it. None is beyond it.

RAY: No.

JAY: You must consider it deeply.

RAY: I know it well. Only because of those things do I live happily, otherwise, you can see the situation of others – in which situation they live. I live in heaven – greater than a hundred heavens.

JAY: You are quite out of the facts of the world.

RAY: You are in this state. You have none – you are issueless. So, you have no practical ideas about such things.

JAY: You forget the days when your body will be placed in a lowly bed keeping you from your all palatial buildings.

RAY: [*Silent.*]

JAY: False tears will be dropped for your loss by your kith and kin. But now you can't understand any thing. Once the time comes, when all understand its fact – what is life and its importance? At last, when everything goes, the man says that life is absurd and you will also say the same. Let the time come.

RAY: No.

JAY: What?

RAY: The real matter is different.

JAY: What is the difference?

RAY: Those who say life is absurd suffer enough in life, otherwise all are happy. I am also happy with life. I thank God, Who has given me life and all other things which I enjoy and live in a state of bliss. I am very fortunate in this regard.

JAY: Whatever you have now, all are false. They are not yours. They are of others.

RAY: I have made all this. I have earned all this. So, I am its real honour.

JAY: [*Laughs.*] Ha...ha.

RAY: What?

JAY: [*Continues to laugh.*] Ha...ha.

JAY: You are not its honour.

RAY: Who is its real honour?

JAY: You are empty-handed and living in a state of delusion which will be shattered at a time which is quite unknown by anyone in the world.

[Shows a 30-second video of a rich man who is dead.]

RAY: I am its honour.

JAY: No.

RAY: Who is its honour?

JAY: All are its temporary honour.

RAY: How?

JAY: You are not its real honour – rather after your death your honour will be nominated another who will also be a temporary honour.

RAY: No.

JAY: I am right.

RAY: You are quite wrong.

JAY: You must know your existence and the meaning of life. Once you will go from here leaving everything. Your hands are empty.

RAY: That is common. There is nothing new in it.

JAY: Yes...yes. Everything is old and told. I say. But you don't admit this fact.

RAY: I do admit.

JAY: You admit that which is on surface level but not that which is hidden.

RAY: What?

JAY: This is a very bitter formula. So, none admits and tries to decline, though impossible.

RAY: What?

JAY: The same that I have told you.

RAY: What?

JAY: 'Zero into plus'.

RAY: What does it mean?

JAY: Life is 'zero into plus' – our life is absurd. All things of the world and man are absurd. Life is an illusion. We are aliens and our home is quite unknown though we always try to know our home. But all go in vain. Beasts have existence and they are part of Nature, but not man. This world is for them.

RAY: How?

JAY: I had a pet dog who behaved very friendly toward me. Its name was 'Inhome'. I used to give food and Inhome used to sleep with me – used to love me – but saying 'Aliensect'. When I came home, Inhome ran towards me and saluted me too. Unfortunately, I fell ill and was admitted to hospital for six months. But when I came back from there, Inhome refused to recognize me and bit me too. I was badly wounded.

RAY: Does Inhome bite you?

JAY: Yes.

RAY: He forgot you?

JAY: Yes.

RAY: Why?

JAY: Because the world is not my home. I live in others' homes. I wish for their friendship – they need not be my friend. I am in search of my existence. But they are living here happily in their home.

RAY: Have you no home?

JAY: Really, I have no home. All have a home, except man.

RAY: Really?

JAY: Yes.

RAY: [*Long pause.*] 'Aliensect' is a very abusive word that was used by Inhome for you.

JAY: I also felt it, but I was compelled to hear.

RAY: You should have left.

JAY: I thought to do so, but I never tried to continue my friendship with Inhome. But all was in vain and once I was bitten by Inhome.

RAY: Let Inhome go.

JAY: I have left.

RAY: Very good.

JAY: [*Pause.*] Whatsoever, but man is here alone and routed out from his home. So, he is always in a state of fear and insecurity – always in search of a home.

RAY: That is not a matter.

JAY: Why?

RAY: My findings are different.

JAY: What?

RAY: The main thing is that whatever I have made or earned is for me and I am its real honour.

JAY: Believe! Know! You are not its real honour. All are absurd. You possess nothing except zero or absurdity.

RAY: I am its real honour and my name is registered everywhere – in every record. None can take my property – none can touch my property without my permission.

JAY: [*Laughs loudly.*] Ha...ha.

RAY: Why?

JAY: Your ideas are fully childish. Are you really a child?

RAY: How? Do you like to humiliate me?

JAY: No...no. You think that none can touch the property in your name.

RAY: Yes...yes.

JAY: This idea is absolutely wrong. You will fail to possess and you all will go in vain automatically.

RAY: How?

JAY: The fact is that you have no existence and one day you will be automatically abandoned from your right – from your property. You will have nothing and you will depart from this place empty-handed.

RAY: [*Silent.*]

JAY: When the fatal time comes, everything disappears within a moment and you will do nothing except accept death.

RAY: [*Long pause.*] Okay. I realize your ideas for a minute. Please tell me what you have and why you do all this. Why do you work for charitable works?

JAY: I have indeed nothing. People say that I am issueless and I accept their ideas happily because this is the fact of the world.

RAY: Are you issueless?

JAY: Yes.

RAY: Really?

JAY: Yes.

RAY: Have you no children?

JAY: No.

RAY: Is your wife alive?

JAY: No.

RAY: What happened to her?

JAY: She was thoroughly ill.

RAY: Was she ill before marriage too?

JAY: Yes.

RAY: What happened to her?

JAY: Multiple diseases in her – from top to bottom. It changed its course and symptoms. There was not one or two – there were no definite symptoms.

RAY: Did you consult doctors?

JAY: Yes.

RAY: Did you?

JAY: Yes...yes – hundreds of doctors.

RAY: What did they say?

JAY: They said that she would be cured and for her treatment, they prescribed several medicines, but she was not cured.

RAY: Was she not cured?

JAY: She was never cured fully.

RAY: Why?

JAY: I can't say.

RAY: Why not?

JAY: Really, when one disease was cured another started. In this way, several diseases affected her.

RAY: It means she was not properly cured.

JAY: Really, she was never cured.

RAY: This was a mistake. Perhaps the doctors failed to diagnose properly.

JAY: The same is said by all others.

RAY: I also think.

JAY: But the same happens to all.

RAY: To all?

JAY: Yes.

RAY: How?

JAY: All are ill. None is fit. The most dangerous disease is death.

RAY: [*Silent.*]

JAY: The same happens to all others.

RAY: No.

JAY: Yes.

RAY: You are not right.

JAY: I am absolutely right but none accepts this fact because all are fools.

RAY: Do you abuse all?

JAY: I don't abuse, but all are abused naturally.

RAY: How?

JAY: Life is abused by death. Death is a natural abuse.

RAY: You are a well-known personality of the city and a man of knowledge, so you should talk responsibly. The eyes of millions of people are on you.

JAY: I know and understand this.

RAY: You must accept your responsibility.

JAY: I do feel – I do work.

RAY: It seems that you have lost faith in God because of personal problems.

JAY: This is not a matter.

RAY: [*Long pause.*] Please tell me. What happened to your family?

JAY: I am a man of Alienland and I am always in search of my own home. My wife departed from here leaving me alone, while she told me and promised during the wedding tie that she would live with me for life. But she left me alone here and she went to an unknown place. I always try to search for her but she is unseen. I spent forty years in search of her, but all went in vain.

RAY: It seems that you had missed managing your family. You should have had care for her, but you missed doing so. This mistake brought you to this state of woes and suffering.

JAY: No.

RAY: Yes.

JAY: All are ill here.

RAY: None.

JAY: All...all.

RAY: You are a pessimist.

JAY: I am not a pessimist.

RAY: You should realize what I know and you don't know.

JAY: I know far better than you.

RAY: You are unnecessarily in a state of overconfidence.

JAY: I say whatever I know.

RAY: You should review your stand. See other people of the world and their happy life.

JAY: I see and know that none are happy here.

RAY: How?

JAY: Who has come here is ill. All are weeping – all are crying. All are dying.

RAY: All who suffer say the same, but the fact is different.

JAY: You are out of track of facts. The fact is that those who don't know the meaning of life say that life is full of pleasure. But once the time comes when all know and leave this world, making life absurd. Lastly, tears are produced in every eye.

RAY: [*Silent.*]

JAY: This is the truth of the world.

RAY: [*Long pause.*] If you have no wife, who will survive you?

JAY: None is survived.

RAY: You will have no existence.

JAY: All go from here without existence.

RAY: No.

JAY: Believe me.

RAY: How can I believe falsehoods?

JAY: Believe me. I am right.

RAY: My condition is quite different. I have two sons. They are millionaires. They will survive me.

JAY: You have also no sons. You are like me. Later or sooner, all go. All die and lose their existence making everything 'zero into plus'.

RAY: How?

JAY: Plus is always an illusion. Plus is a very dangerous word but very attractive for all mankind.

RAY: What do you say?

JAY: All move around it, but once everything becomes zero. So, life is 'zero into plus'. Man follows 'plus' but gets 'zero'. But it is unfelt till the end comes.

RAY: No. This is not a matter.

JAY: Believe, this is the only matter. The world moves around this. It cheats all and makes life absurd.

RAY: There is an end to everything. But it doesn't mean that life is absurd.

JAY: This is the eternal fact. All are under the same formula of 'zero into four'.

RAY: How?

JAY: Remember your forefathers. What happened to them? They all are gone. What was the meaning of their life?

RAY: I know and understand. They left us but their name and fame are glorified with their deeds and virtues.

JAY: There is no value of anything for them who are no more in this world.

RAY: [Silent.]

JAY: Nothing in this world can respect them. Can an honour voice awaken them? Can flowery graves give them life? Can incense sticks give breath to their bodies? Can awards and trophies bring them back to us?

[Shows a 1-minute video of a graveyard.]

RAY: [Silent.]

JAY: Know and understand. Nothing in the world can awaken those who are dead.

RAY: This is the divine fact, but they are survived by us. But you will be survived by none.

JAY: You will also be survived by none like me. All are alike.

RAY: All are not alike. All are different.

JAY: Know, my friend, all are alike.

RAY: How can you say?

JAY: Whether rich or poor, all are the same.

RAY: How?

JAY: All live in the land of woes and sorrows expecting joy which is never fulfilled.

RAY: Someone may live, but not all.

JAY: All live in the same land – in the death land.

RAY: [*Silent.*]

JAY: But all fail to know and understand the reality of the world and people.

RAY: No. I am not like you – I am not like others.

JAY: Life is itself a very tough subject and very few people know it. If you wish to know, listen to the lyric.

RAY: Yes. Sing.

JAY: [*Sings.*]

Life in this dry and Godless world is vain
But in the same state, all live in.
All wait for divine bliss to be dropped
But death drops making life earth-led.

Life in this dry and Godless world is vain –
And our souls leave the chamber breaking chain.
Of course, the best award of life is death,
Although unfelt by all till they lose their faith.

Lights down.

Act 3

Lights up.

DON *enters. An announcement is heard.*

An announcement is heard. 'Pilgrims, attention, please! There is free food and lodging available from Aliet Charitable Trust. All are requested to avail themselves of the vegetarian food and lodging facilities.

DON: Greetings, great men of charity! Greeting the men of values and virtues!

[*Enters.*]

RAY: Welcome!

JAY: Most welcome!

DON: Can you not allow me a blanket?

RAY: Are you a pilgrim?

DON: Yes.

RAY: Okay. You must go to the counter and stand in the queue. One blanket will be served to everyone.

JAY: Yes. The counter will open in ten minutes.

DON: May I pass this time here?

JAY: My pleasure! I am at your service. Sit down.

DON: Thanks.

RAY: From where have you come?

DON: I have come here from Bulletland.

RAY: Where is this place?

DON: It is on the southern side.

RAY: I have never heard the name of this place.

DON: It may be, but most people know it.

RAY: Really, I don't know it.

DON: You may know it easily once you fall under this area anyhow.

RAY: I don't like to go there.

DON: All go there one day – happily or unhappily.

RAY: I don't go anywhere.

DON: You will also go.

RAY: No.

DON: Wait for the proper time.

RAY: I am sure I don't go there. I have never heard of or seen this place.

DON: This is not a matter. Whether you see it or not – you will have to go there. All go. All meet me one day.

RAY: [*Pause.*] Where is this place?

DON: This is just opposite Thorns Hill.

RAY: Any popular thing about this place you may say?

DON: Yes.

RAY: Tell me.

DON: This place is famous for graveyards and crematoria.

RAY: For graveyards and crematoria?

DON: Yes.

RAY: Not for temples and churches or mosques or any other holy places?

DON: Very few, but they are also connected to some graveyards and crematoria.

RAY: They are also connected?

DON: Yes.

RAY: Also?

DON: Yes...yes.

[*JAY joins them.*]

JAY: Right...right. You are quite right.

RAY: What?

JAY: Temples also have crematoria – mosques and churches also have graveyards.

DON: Really, there is not even a single religious place where there are no graveyards and crematoria.

JAY: Crematoria and graveyards are the holiest places.

DON: I know well. I am their keeper.

RAY: This is everywhere. All know.

JAY: But all are afraid of these places.

RAY: This is not a matter. God manages everything and for His management all this is.

DON: There is no God. God is hope which is never seen and witnessed.

RAY: Are you a pilgrim?

DON: Yes.

RAY: Why do you say all this in this place of God?

DON: It is common. This is absolutely true.

RAY: No. This is not common. I know God and His power. You also know, so you have come here.

DON: No...no.

RAY: Why not?

DON: I have come here as a pilgrim like all others but I know that there is no God. The world is Godless.

RAY: Then why have you come here?

DON: Like all others.

RAY: But they believe in God.

DON: But I don't.

RAY: You will go to hell.

DON: [*Laughs.*] Ha...ha.

RAY: Why are you satirizing God?

DON: There is no God. I am myself a determiner of all men and women who come to this world.

RAY: How?

DON: I don't like to say.

RAY: Tell me.

DON: You will hate me if you know.

RAY: Tell me. I will not hate you.

DON: I am a robber – I am a killer. I rob the life of man – I rob everything of man – for me another's life is zero – for me life is a plaything.

RAY: Life is zero for you?

DON: Yes...yes.

RAY: Are you the god of death?

DON: [*Silent.*]

RAY: Tell us.

DON: Let the time come.

RAY: Have you no mercy?

DON: There is no mercy in the world.

RAY: You should think about your evil deeds.

DON: My deeds are pure.

RAY: [*Silent.*]

DON: I purify the world honestly. For me all are equal. For me, there is no difference between the rich and the poor – between young and old – between men and women – between ugly and charming. All are the same for me. I have been fulfilling my duty very honestly since the beginning. I never sleep.

RAY: Why do you do all this?

DON: This is my profession.

RAY: Is this your profession?

DON: Yes.

RAY: Do you do all this with pilgrims?

DON: Yes.

RAY: Are you not afraid of God?

DON: [*Laughs.*] Ha...ha...ha.

RAY: You are really a mean man. You are a criminal. I will call the police.

DON: There are no police.

RAY: There are thousands of police posted here.

DON: None will come to arrest me.

RAY: Why?

DON: They don't come because I pay all of them?

RAY: Do you pay all of them from the spoils of robbery?

DON: Yes.

DON: Do the police help you in such deeds?

DON: Yes...yes.

RAY: Have they no character and shame?

DON: None has shame. All go unclothed. When they depart from here, they have no clothes.

RAY: Really, you are a shame to the earth – you are a burden on this earth.

DON: There is no shame in this world – there is no burden on this earth. All merge into this earth.

RAY: But I am not a man who robs or kills. I donate millions of dollars to this trust every year for the help of the pilgrims. I have done this for the last forty years. So, God has given me everything. I live happily. I am the richest man in the country.

DON: [*Laughingly.*] There is no God. God is only hoping which is never fulfilled.

RAY: Believe. There is God, Who commands all of us. You are also under the same command.

DON: There is nothing in God's name. That is only an illusion. So, that is not a matter to be afraid of in any way.

RAY: Believe. Once, God will penalize you – once the police will penalize you. You will suffer.

DON: No, I will never suffer.

RAY: Your place will be in hell. Devils will torture you there.

DON: [*Laughs.*] Ha...ha...ha.

RAY: Wait for God's judgement.

DON: Either good or bad all have the same consequences. No differences in any way.

RAY: No.

DON: You will have to face the same.

JAY: Don is right. All have the same condition. All will embrace death – either one is right or wrong.

RAY: God delivers His judgement according to the deeds which we do.

DON: [*Laughs.*] Ha...ha.

RAY: No difference?

DON: No. I have killed several people. I have robbed several people but no sin to be – no judgement has come against me.

RAY: [*Silent.*]

DON: I fulfil my duty honestly and impartially.

RAY: How brutally do you do all this?

DON: Very happily. This is my duty.

RAY: What do you use for doing so?

DON: I keep several things to rob and kill – different ways for different persons at different times.

RAY: Be sure. Your place will be reserved in hell.

DON: [*Laughs.*] Ha...ha...ha.

RAY: None can save from God's eyes.

DON: Nothing will happen to me. I determine the fate of all people. I have its eternal licence. It need not to be renewed. It never expires. But man expires.

[*An announcement is heard. 'Pilgrims and residents, attention, please! The administration imposes a curfew order on the city because of serial bomb blasts in different places and the slaying of nearly seventy thousand people. None are allowed out of their house, because the operation against the militants by the police is ongoing. Militants are hiding in the city.'*

JAY *switches on the television and all three watch it.*]

RAY: What happened? Listen to the news bulletin.

JAY: [*Slowly.*] Annihilation! All are lost. All is gone.

DON: Really, now right and wrong became equal. All become equal.

RAY: [*Seriously.*] Our life is in danger. I think now our life will expire.

JAY: All will go in vain.

DON: If they begin to fire at militants, the bullets may injure you – you might be killed.

JAY: Listen to the news bulletin.

RAY: The militants are hiding in the trust's building. The police personnel have barricaded it. Firing has begun.

DON: The bullet may reach you unintentionally. You might be killed.

RAY: Any solution?

JAY: Can you not pray to God for His help?

RAY: [*Sadly.*] Is God our servant? How will He come here to save? In such a situation of fear and terror, how can I pray to God for His help?

DON: [*Silent.*]

RAY: [*Sadly.*] Have you no bullets?

DON: Yes, I have sufficient bullets.

RAY: Can you take us to a safe place?

DON: Yes.

RAY: [*Sadly.*] Please help us soon.

DON: Why are you anxious?

RAY: [*Dejectedly.*] My all family members arrived here last night and they had to go to the House of God for His blessings at twelve o'clock.

DON: Very good. Let them stay.

RAY: [*Sadly.*] But I don't know how they are?

DON: Let them stay. Remain tension free.

RAY: [*Sadly.*] I feel uneasiness now.

DON: Why?

RAY: [*Sadly.*] I can't give a proper reason.

DON: Avoid such feelings.

RAY: [*Sadly.*] I am trying to do so but in vain.

DON: When the curfew ends, you will know their condition.

RAY: [*Sadly.*] When will the curfew be withdrawn?

DON: I think within some minutes.

RAY: [*Sadly.*] How?

DON: Because the city is full of pilgrims. So, the commander will not detain them here for a long time.

RAY: [*Sadly.*] God knows. What will happen?

DON: The same, which happens to all.

RAY: [*Sadly.*] Any easy way to escape from here?

JAY: If befriended with the zero, it is possible.

RAY: [*Sadly.*] How?

JAY: Making life zero into plus.

RAY: Oh! Bullets begin to pierce the walls of this room too.

DON: Yes.

RAY: Now how can we save our life?

JAY: Impossible.

[*There is a news bulletin on the screen of television. JAY, RAY, and DON are watching the screen.*]

JAY: Listen to the news bulletin.

NEWSREADER: [*On the television screen.*] The most shocking news! All the members of Ray's family have been killed in the bomb blast in Hotel Aliet, where they were staying. Their bodies have been just recovered. Ray is also staying here. He is the only man who used to donate a maximum amount for the charitable works in this city for about twenty years. He is the only man in the country who used to donate money for charitable works. The whole country salutes him and prays to God to give him the patience to bear the agony caused by the untimely death of his family members. On the other hand, the police have failed to track any militants and none has been arrested until now.

RAY: [*Weeps.*] Oh...oh! All of my family members who were staying in the Hotel Aliet have been killed in the bomb blasts.

JAY: It seems that we will not save ourselves from this condition because the firing has begun at our office and it is announced by the administration that militants are hiding in another cell of this office and have captured some pilgrims who they plan to kill.

DON: [*Silent.*]

RAY: [*Weeps.*]

JAY: Oh! Oh! The bullet pierced Ray. He's fallen to the ground. He is dying. Oh! Oh!

RAY: Oh my God...oh...oh...m...y...G...o...d!

[*The bullet pierces. Falls. Covered with blood.*]

DON: Let him go to his own home. You will also go.

JAY: Oh! Oh...!

[*Falls. Covered with blood.*]

DON: Peace and peace for you now.

[*Disappears suddenly.*]

A song entitled 'Life is zero into plus...' is heard from an unknown direction.

Life is a 'zero into plus' show,
But all think of it as a huge glow.
Each one wishes to handle plus,
Although ever changes into a flush.

Life is a shade and the earth made
Though none accepts life as a shade
And all move towards the old trend
Nearing the deep, low, and cold yard.

Wining wearies, then miseries
But feeling one is gaining joys.
Life is a vow – never to glow,
Life is a 'zero into plus' show.

Lights down.

www.ingramcontent.com/pod-product-compliance
Lightning Source LLC
Chambersburg PA
CBHW071457280626
47160CB00023B/2124